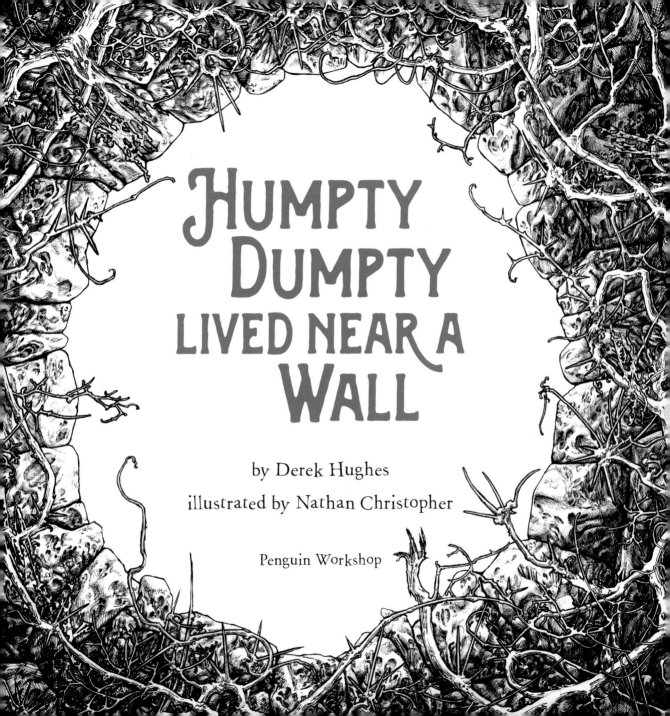

Humpty Dumpty Lived Near a Wall

by Derek Hughes

illustrated by Nathan Christopher

Penguin Workshop

PENGUIN WORKSHOP
An Imprint of Penguin Random House LLC, New York

Text copyright © 2020 by Derek Hughes. Illustrations copyright © 2020 by Nathan Christopher. All rights reserved. Published by Penguin Workshop, an imprint of Penguin Random House LLC, New York. PENGUIN and PENGUIN WORKSHOP are trademarks of Penguin Books Ltd, and the W colophon is a registered trademark of Penguin Random House LLC. Manufactured in China.

Visit us online at www.penguinrandomhouse.com.

Library of Congress Cataloging-in-Publication Data is available upon request.

ISBN 9781524793029   10 9 8 7 6 5 4 3 2 1

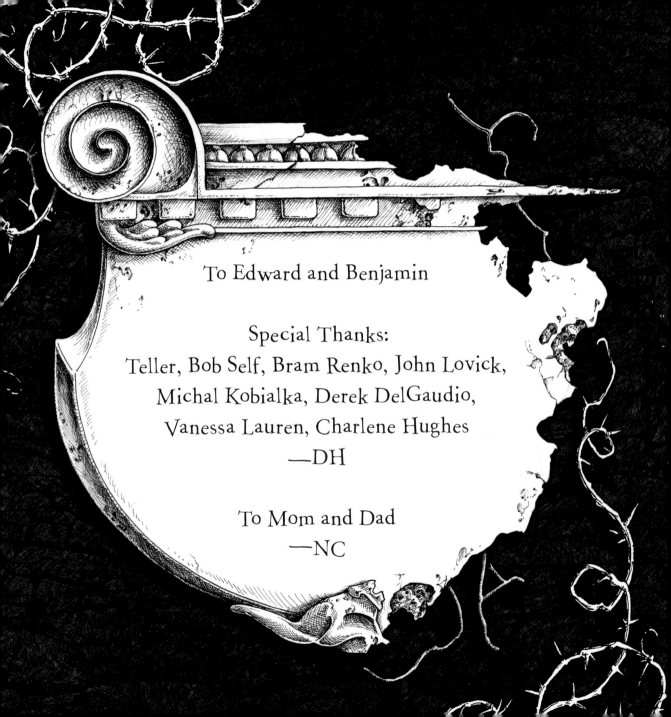

To Edward and Benjamin

Special Thanks:
Teller, Bob Self, Bram Renko, John Lovick,
Michal Kobialka, Derek DelGaudio,
Vanessa Lauren, Charlene Hughes
—DH

To Mom and Dad
—NC

Humpty Dumpty lived near a wall.

Humpty Dumpty
had no fun at all.

He worked all day long
under fluorescent light,

and due to back pain,
couldn't sleep
through the night.

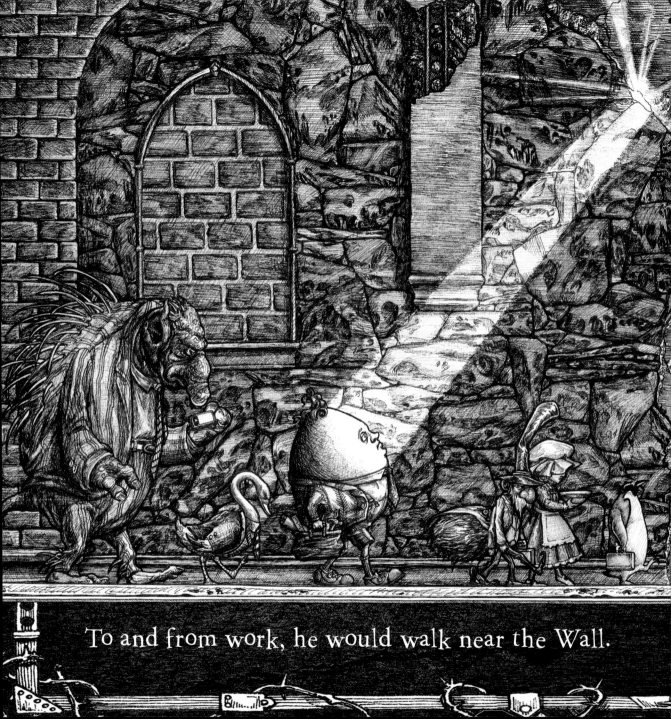

To and from work, he would walk near the Wall.

Days lived in shadows, that Wall was so tall.

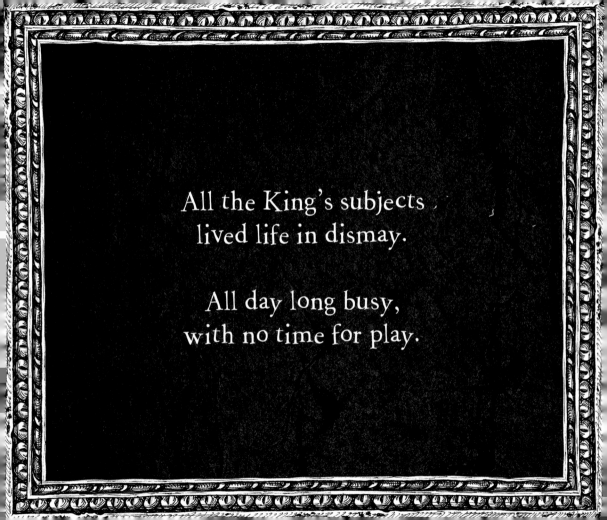

All the King's subjects
lived life in dismay.

All day long busy,
with no time for play.

The King had forbidden
his empire to dream.
Keep everyone working,
his self-serving scheme.

But a vision had hatched,
and it was no joke.
If the King knew his plan,
he'd scramble his yolk.

He kept his dream quiet,
told no one at all.

His secret ambition?
Look over the Wall.

He couldn't even tell his friend the Mad Hatter.
To realize his dream . . .

he was building a ladder.

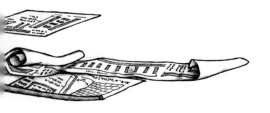

Ladder complete,
he stole into the night,
avoiding King's men
and hiding from sight.

Fear pushed to the side.

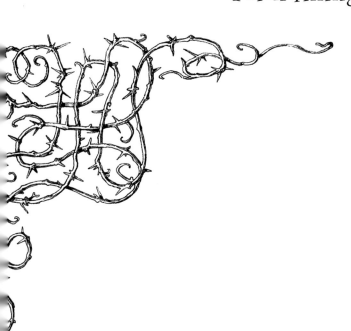

Faith filling his lungs.

Hand over hand,
he climbed up the rungs.

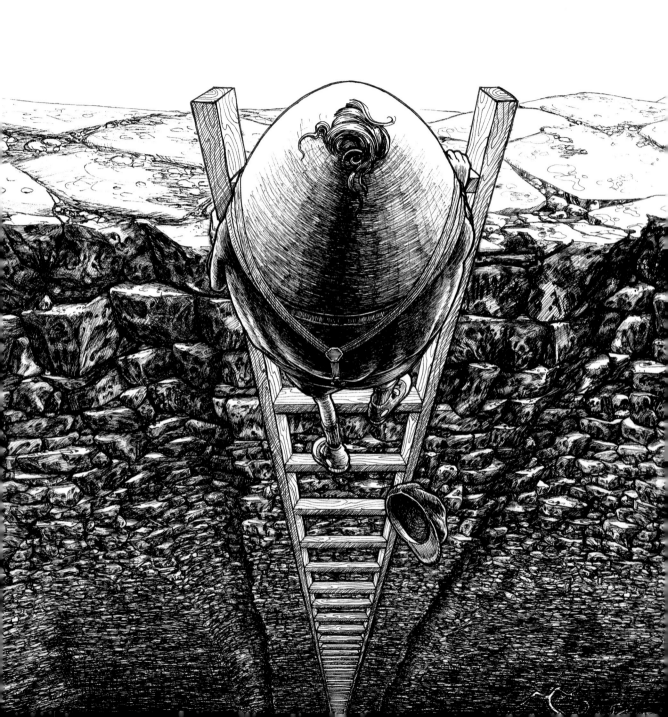

The next morning, at daybreak . . .

news spread to the rest.

Someone in the kingdom put the Wall to the test.
The headlines that day said the Wall had won out.

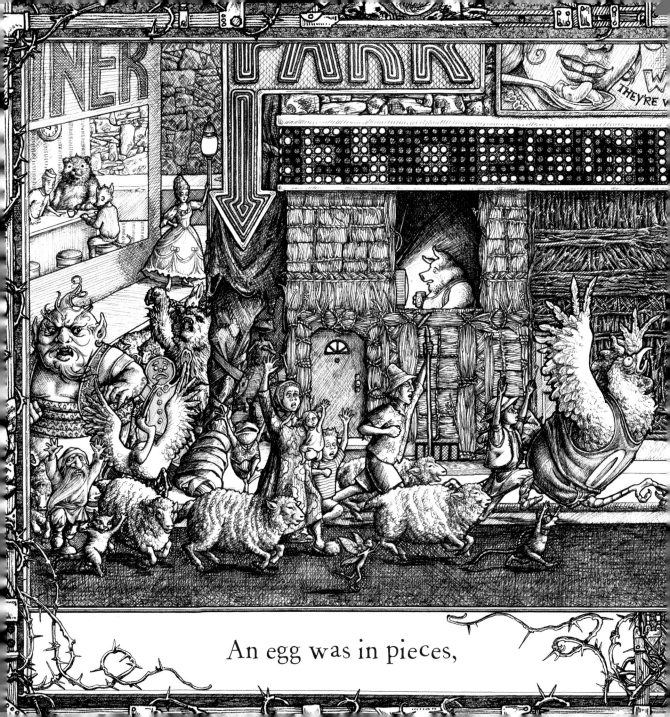

An egg was in pieces,

so tragic,

no doubt.

To stop other subjects from
changing their fate,
and to prove to his realm
that dreams aren't so great,

the King sent a photo
to one and to all,
the remains of an egg
at the foot of the Wall.

But the King and his men had missed something new.
That photo was proof the egg's dreams had come true.

On broken eggshells, pushed in a great pile . . .
one piece was on top,

that piece had a smile.

The End

When **Derek Hughes** was ten years old,
he had open-heart surgery. Later that year, he
decided that when he grew up, he would become
a magician. Now all grown up, he performs his
magic for audiences all over the world. He lives
with his family in Minneapolis, Minnesota.

www.standupmagician.com
Twitter: @standupmagician
Instagram: standupmagician

Nathan Christopher studied Art and Drama at the
University of Minnesota. As an artist he has created artwork,
installations, and designs for theater and other arts groups,
commercial businesses, and individual patrons, and has
won several national arts competitions. Nathan is also an
award-winning actor and has appeared on many of the
stages in his hometown of Minneapolis and toured with
companies in the United States, Europe, and Russia.

nathanchristopher.net